Paperboy 2: Overwhelming Odds

By Omari Jeremiah

MORTON BOOKS, Inc.

FIRST MORTON BOOKS EDITION
Copyright 2005, Omari Jeremiah
Second Printing, 2007

Morton ISBN:1-929188-10-2
Cover design by Bernie Rollins
www.robmorton.com

Printed in the United States of America

This book is dedicated to Aquisha Jeremiah, Mommy, Daddy, Osei and my Aunt Pat. Thank you for your ideas and support.

Contents

An evil organization falls.

A hero has won!

Or so we thought.........

After Paperboy defeated ScizzorMan, he had his mind set on the destruction of LOEP (The League of Evil People). However, before he could destroy the evil organization, LOEP struck back with more force than Paperboy could handle. To make matters worse, an enemy that is virtually impossible to defeat has arrived at Paperboy's school to capture him: a teacher. If this was not bad enough, Paperboy finds himself as prey for a hunter that wishes to destroy him. Can Paperboy defeat these three powerful enemies? Or will his enemies overwhelm him?

Chapter 1
The Principal's Announcement

ONE

"Michael! Get ready for school!"

"Okay mom!" Michael replied.

"I'm leaving on a business trip! I'll be back in five days! Breakfast is on the table!"

"Okay mom."

"Have a good day!"

"Bye Mom!"

Michael got up from his bed and stretched. He tried to do this every morning. It was a little workout before he went to school. At school, he got a workout he never wanted: capturing bullies, stopping bullies from pushing around the gossiping girls, game whiz boys, and nerds, and foiling bullies plans to destroy him. Being a school hero was not easy.

Michael thought about what happened two weeks ago. He thought about Shorty Scarface and ScizzorMan. He thought about Paper Blade boomerangs and the four groups at recess at PS 266. Everyone at PS 266 seemed to have friends. Everyone except Michael. Michael had no time to make friends. He was always too busy being Paperboy. Sometimes Michael wished he was a normal kid. But Michael had gone too far down the path he had chosen. Going back was not an option.

"I guess I'll just have to get use to being alone," Michael said sadly.

With a heavy sigh, Michael started getting ready to go to school. He took a shower, got dressed, and went downstairs for breakfast. After breakfast, he put on his paper mask and cape and took the PaperMobile out of the garage. Paperboy then rode to school. The paper lasers and paper airplanes were still on his bike. He had not removed them since he first put them on. Once at PS 266, he chained the PaperMobile to the school's gate and put a pad lock on it. Paperboy then dashed to the janitor's closet and changed. Michael walked out of the janitor's closet. Just when Michael was about to enter his classroom, an announcement came on the loudspeaker. It was the principal.

"Attention all students and teachers! Please report to the playground area! We have new students!"'

"No," Michael groaned.

Mr. Pride, the principal, always did this when PS 266 had new students. Mr. Pride felt every student was special; he felt the school was one big family. New students to him were new members of his family, and they should be introduced to school in a special way.

Everyone moved into the playground. They circled around the new students and the principal. The principal started speaking.

"We have three new students!" Mr. Pride said excitedly.

"This is James," Mr. Pride said, pointing to a dark skinned boy who looked like he was around Michael's age.

"This is Nina," Mr. Pride said pointing to a light skinned girl with long dark hair. She looked like she was around Michael's age too.

"And last but not least, this is Billy," Mr. Pride said pointing to a small light skinned boy with untamed hair and a grin Michael did not like. Billy looked younger than Michael.

"I also have one more surprise before you all go back to class. We have a new teacher! Everyone meet Mr. Raptor!"

Mr. Raptor was a tall man with mean, dark eyes. He stared at the crowd in disgust and then looked towards the ground. Michael was surprised he did not notice Mr. Raptor before.

"Would any of you like to say anything?" Mr. Pride asked.

"I would!" shouted Billy.

Mr. Pride gave the stage to Billy. Billy cleared his throat. "I have nothing to say," he announced with a grin.

Mr. Pride raised an eyebrow at Billy. "Please return to class," he said.

Everyone returned to their classes. When Michael got into his seat in his classroom, he noticed Miss Rex had a bad cough. Other than that, class continued and ended as it normally did.

Uneventful.

After class, Michael dashed into the janitor's closet and changed. Paperboy ran outside, ready to face any evil that threatened him. Oddly, no bullies were pushing people around. In fact, Paperboy didn't see any bullies. He thought of reasons how this could be possible. And then he knew why there were no bullies in the playground. Max Parker was suspended from school the day Paperboy defeated ScizzorMan. *That suspension*, Paperboy thought trembling, *ends tomorrow*.

Chapter 2

The Paper Claw

TWO

After school was over that day, Mr. Raptor walked into Mr. Pride's office.

"Is there anything I can do for you, Mr. Raptor?" The principal asked, looking up from the pile of papers on his desk.

"We have a problem," Mr. Raptor replied.

"What's wrong?"

"The question is, what is wrong with you, Mr. Pride?" Mr. Raptor asked angrily.

Mr. Pride was somewhat taken aback both by the question and Mr. Raptor's tone of voice. "What do you mean by that?"

"Do you know the situation at recess?" Mr. Raptor asked.

"Yes."

"Do you know about Paperboy?"

"Yes."

"Have you captured him?"

"Why would I want to do that?" Mr. Pride asked.

"He's attacking other students!" Mr. Raptor roared.

"Paperboy has been capturing the troublemakers of this school; and from what I have heard, he's also stopped plans to hurt or kill fellow students," Mr. Pride said calmly.

"But he's doing just that to other students," Mr. Raptor argued. "Our school guards are supposed to stop troublemakers; not a boy in a costume! This makes your school seem dysfunctional. In addition to that, Paperboy is a troublemaker himself! Some of your students are scared Paperboy will hurt them. Eventually they will stay home from school and will not get the proper education their parents paid for. Is this what you want, Mr. Pride?"

"No," Mr. Pride answered. "But Paperboy has also saved…"

"This is why we need to capture Paperboy!" Mr. Raptor interrupted. "If we don't, there's no future for the kids who attend PS 266. If you give me one chance, I can capture Paperboy and prove how evil this boy's intentions are."

"Fine," Mr. Pride said. "I'll give you one chance. If you fail, never talk to me about Paperboy again. Understand?"

"I understand. I'll catch him during recess. I just need your consent to control recess."

"You have my permission," Mr. Pride said.

"Good," Mr. Raptor replied. The angry voice was now gone, replaced by a upbeat tone.

Mr. Raptor departed from the principal's office and went home to plan his capture of Paperboy.

Meanwhile, Michael sat up in his bed, nervous. He was positive Shorty Scarface was going to try to get revenge. However, he did not know what Shorty could do now that the dreaded ScizzorMan was gone.

Shorty will come up with something. Michael thought. *I have to be ready.*

Just then, an idea came to Michael. An enemy could take away Michael's paper airplanes, paper lasers, and Paper Blade Boomerangs (PBB's). Maybe this is what Shorty was planning. Michael needed a weapon that nobody could take away. Maybe something on his fingers. Michael thought of a glove. Then he thought of a claw.

"That's it!" Michael exclaimed. "I'll make a Paper Claw! It will be a Paper glove with sharp edges on the fingertips. This way I'll always have a weapon!"

Michael started constructing the "Paper Claw" right away. He made a paper glove with sharp edges on the fingertips. The first Paper Claw did not fit Michael's hand, but this did not discourage him. After two long hours, Michael had finally constructed two perfect Paper Claws. The claws fit Michael's hands; and almost cut him when he dared to touch the tip. He eventually was able to construct more user friendly paper claws. Soon Michael could construct a good pair of paper claws in five minutes.

After making fifty Paper Claws, Michael went to bed. It was late and he would need all the rest he could get for tomorrow. Michael felt prepared to face Shorty Scarface and the bullies tomorrow. Little did he know just how unprepared he really was.

THREE

When Michael got up the next morning, he felt drowsy. Making the Paper Claw had its consequences. Michael stretched, took a shower, got dressed, went downstairs, made breakfast, ate breakfast, and changed into his Paperboy costume. Paperboy then rode to school on the PaperMobile.

Once he was at PS 266, Paperboy chained the PaperMobile to the gate and put a pad lock on it. He then ran to the janitor's closet and changed. Michael walked out of the janitor's closet. As Michael walked toward his classroom, he noticed a little boy across the hall crying. Curiosity overcame him and he went over to the little boy.

Suddenly, the little boy tackled Michael to the floor.

"Tag! You're it!" The boy declared.

"What do you think you're doing?" Michael asked angrily.

The boy looked at Michael, and Michael recognized him.

"You're the new kid!" Michael exclaimed.

" I'm Billy!" The boy shouted excitedly.

"Get off of me!" Michael said curtly.

The boy jumped to his feet and started hopping around. Michael could tell sugar had claimed another victim. Michael got up. "Are you okay?," he said.

"I'm lonely,." the boy said. "This school is boring. Will you be my friend?

Michael looked at Billy, and then looked at a nearby clock.

"I'm late for class!"

Michael couldn't believe it. He had never been late for class before. Billy just stood there, and then started hopping up and down and smiling.

"Out of my way!"

Michael pushed Billy to the floor and tried to open the door to his classroom. But before he could, Billy grabbed his foot and pulled him to the floor.

"Hi! My name is Billy Howard! What's yours?"

Michael was furious now. He kicked Billy in the face and got up. Billy tried to pull him down again but Michael kicked Billy again, harder than the last time, and Billy fell on his back. Thinking quickly, Michael ran to his nearby classroom and turned the doorknob. Before he could push it open, Billy tackled him again.

"What is your name?" Billy asked angrily.

"Michael! Now leave me alone!" Michael bellowed.

"Are we friends, Michael?" Billy asked, a smile creeping on his face.

"Never!"

Michael pushed Billy off of him and stood up. Billy got up and raced to Michael's classroom door.

"Step away from the door, Billy." Michael demanded angrily.

Billy smiled and grabbed Michael's knapsack. Suddenly, Michael fell to the floor. Michael looked up. He could not believe what he saw. Billy was dragging him by his knapsack! The same knapsack that had all of Michael's paper masks, capes, and accessories! Michael had to stop Billy and get to class. Michael lifted his arms up, which parted him from his knapsack. He then quickly stood up and tripped Billy. Billy fell and dropped Michael's knapsack.

Michael picked it up quickly and ran to his classroom. He turned around to see if Billy was chasing after him. Instead he saw two protractors at each side of the hall. Billy stood up and ran after Michael. Once his foot was between the two protractors, the protractors dashed to Billy's foot. The protractors pierced Billy's foot. While the protractors were in Billy's foot, ropes started coming out of them. The ropes bounded Billy's whole body tightly, making Billy immobile and causing him to fall. Michael quickly took advantage of this opportunity and dashed to class.

When he entered the room, Michael was surprised to see Mr. Raptor in front of the chalkboard. An empty chalkboard.

"You must be Michael," Mr. Raptor said. "Sit down. I will do you a favor if you do me a favor."

Michael sat down and listened.

"Tell me all you know about Paperboy, and I won't mark you late."

Michael was surprised. The one person he knew best could get him back his perfect record. Michael answered, "He uses a special weapon to strike down evil."

"What kind of weapon?" Mr. Raptor asked.

" Paper," Michael simply answered.

This continued for 45 minutes. Mr. Raptor asked many different questions about Paperboy. After that it was time for recess. Michael changed in the janitor's closet. Paperboy then ran out in the playground ready to face Shorty Scarface. Instead he found all the kids on one side of the playground.

"What's going on?" Paperboy wondered.

Paperboy was armed with everything. He had two paper airplanes between his pointer and middle fingers, two PBB's under his pointer finger on each hand, two paper lasers in his pockets, and two paper claws, one on each hand. Paperboy walked out to the crowd.

"We got you!" A familiar voice exclaimed. Paperboy turned around to face Mr. Raptor.

"What's going on Mr. Raptor?" Paperboy asked.

Mr. Raptor smiled and said. "Get him."

All of a sudden, school guards stepped out from the crowd and ran towards Paperboy.

"Your reign of evil ends now, Paperboy." Mr. Raptor declared.

Paperboy was confused. Suddenly a school guard tripped Paperboy. Paperboy fell to the ground with a thud. One thing was clear: the school guards did not want to talk. He had to get away from them and find out what was going on. Paperboy rolled away from the school guard, stood up, and ran.

There were ten school guards chasing him. Paperboy turned around and threw two PBB's at two school guards. The school guards stopped, crying out in pain. Paperboy took out his paper lasers and fired at the ground. Four school guards slipped on the paper balls and fell. Paperboy fired more paper balls but the school guards evaded the paper balls. Paperboy then threw his paper lasers at the school guards, hitting two in the head, forcing them to fall. Then a school guard grabbed Paperboy from the back while two school guards ran up to him. Paperboy struggled to free himself but he couldn't.

Then he remembered the Paper Claw. Paperboy punctured the school guard's wrist that was holding him. As the school guard reacted to this attack, Paperboy freed himself and kicked the school guard to the ground. The last two school guards were tall. Paperboy stood on a school guard's foot for balance and cut the other school guard with a paper airplane.

Paperboy ran for the PaperMobile, with one school guard chasing him. Paperboy unlocked the PaperMobile and fired many paper balls at the school guard's face. Unable to endure the paper balls any longer, the school guard surrendered and fell to the ground.

Now victorious over the school guards, Paperboy pedaled to Mr. Raptor.

"What is this about?" Paperboy asked.

Mr. Raptor just smiled sinisterly and said, "Goodbye, Paperboy."

All of a sudden thirty school guards came rushing out of the crowd and ran toward Paperboy. Paperboy pedaled away from Mr. Raptor and out of PS 266; the school guards were still following him. The harder Paperboy pedaled, the less school guards chased him, until there were none left.

"They must have a given up," Paperboy thought.

As he rode the PaperMobile home, he thought about everything that happened today. With each event was a series of unanswered questions.

"I hope they won't remain unanswered for long," Paperboy thought.

Chapter 4
Michael's New Friends

FOUR

An hour later that day, Michael decided to lay on his bed, his head bursting with questions.

Why was Mr. Raptor after me?

What really happened to the school guards that chased me away from PS 266?

Where did those protractors come from in the hall?

How did those protractors do what they did to Billy?

What's wrong with Billy?

Michael's head felt like it was going to pop.

Ding! Dong! It was the doorbell.

Who could that be? Michael wondered.

Michael went to the door and opened it. Outside was the new kid at school, James.

"Can I help you?" Michael asked.

"No time," James replied quickly. "My name is James Range Pace. I go to your school, PS 266."

"Yeah I know you," Michael replied. "But what do you want?"

"Haven't you had some problems lately, Michael? I know what is wrong. I'm here to help you. May I come in?"

Michael didn't know what to say. All the answers to his questions were right in front of him.

"Come in," Michael managed to say.

"Wait!"

Running up to Michael's door was a light-skinned girl with long dark hair. It was Nina!

"I'm with James," Nina said as she lightly pushed Michael to the side and entered his house.

Michael allowed James to come in and closed the door.

"Follow me," Michael said.

Michael led James and Nina to his room and allowed them to sit on his bed. Michael sat on the floor. James cleared his throat and started speaking.

"First of all, we know you are Paperboy."

Michael was alarmed. "How?" he asked.

"Nina is in your class. She sits in back of you. Once we found out about Paperboy, we both decided to try to figure out his true identity. It didn't take us long for us to find out it was you, Michael. One thing that shouldn't be made out of paper is your mask. Anyway, we found out that Mr. Raptor is trying to capture you. Thanks to my new invention, we were able to listen to Mr. Raptor's conversation with Mr. Pride and..."

"He doesn't want to hear that!" Nina interrupted. "Let me tell the story."

James folded his arms angrily. Nina continued.

"We found out Mr. Raptor wanted to capture you. He thought you were trying to ruin the education of the students at PS 266. Because of what you did for the other three groups two weeks ago, we decided to help you."

"What happened to Billy Howard?" Michael asked.

"I can answer that," James said triumphantly.

"Billy was caught in my 'Protractor Trap.' You see Michael, I can manipulate protractors the same way you can manipulate paper. As you know, protractors are mathematical tools that are used to plot lines and draw them. Nina can manipulate pens. Using laser technology, I caused the two protractors to pierce Billy's foot. I also caused the ropes to immobilize Billy."

"Wow," Michael said. "That's pretty cool."

"Thank you," James replied happily.

"And remember when those school guards chased you out of PS 266 and down the street? Nina used her "waterpen", which is a pen modified to shoot pressurized water, to shoot the school guards and make them slip and fall."

"Cool," Michael said.

Nina took a bow. "Thank you," She replied.

"There's just one more thing I don't understand," Michael said. "Why did Billy attack me?"

"We have enough proof to believe Billy is insane. He is unpredictable. You were just at the wrong place at the wrong time. You were lucky I had to go to the bathroom!" James joked.

Michael laughed. He was satisfied now. Nina looked around Michael's room. Then she spotted a toy in the corner of Michael's room.

"Is that the limited-edition Super Monkey 8000?" Nina asked.

"Yeah," Michael answered. "I bought it recently.......... but I haven't had time to play with it. Being Paperboy isn't easy."

"I can imagine," James said. "And you can't back out of it now."

"I have the Super Monkey 9000." Nina said, changing the subject.

"Really?" Michael asked. "I heard only five were made in the US."

"I can make my own Super Monkey," James added. "With any design you want."

"Cool!" Michael exclaimed.

Michael, James, and Nina talked about many different things. Nina also hit Michael with a pillow and started a pillow fight! James and

Nina stayed at Michael's home for three hours. Michael learned James was smart and creative. He also learned Nina was a little bossy and liked to talk. When James and Nina finally left Michael's house, James told Michael the most reassuring words Michael had heard in a long time:

"You're not alone, pal."

Michael went up to his room happily. He lay down on his bed and prepared to go to sleep. Michael closed his eyes. Then Michael's eyes popped open. He forgot to ask James the question that was disturbing him the most.

What happened to Shorty Scarface?

Chapter 5
Shorty Scarface's Revenge

FIVE

The next day Michael got up earlier than usual. He wondered if he should go back to sleep. After some thought, Michael decided not to go to sleep. Maybe if he went to school earlier as Paperboy, he could persuade Mr. Pride to stop Mr. Raptor from capturing him. Or maybe he could speak to Mr. Raptor himself. With this idea in mind, Michael started getting ready for school.

Michael did his usual morning stretching exercise, took a shower, got dressed, made breakfast, ate breakfast, and changed into his Paperboy costume. Paperboy took out the PaperMobile from the garage and rode to PS 266. He then chained the PaperMobile to the gate and put a pad lock on it. Just when Paperboy was about to enter his school, someone grabbed him from behind.

He managed to free himself and face his attacker. When Paperboy saw his attacker, he was very angry. It was Billy. Billy pushed Paperboy to the floor and started choking him.

"You must be Paperboy," Billy said happily. "Be my friend."

Paperboy ripped Billy's hands off his neck and kicked Billy away from him. He had to talk to Mr. Pride or Mr. Raptor before school started. He had to get away from Billy. To make matters worse, Paperboy had no weapons. He had come to talk, not fight.

Determined to accomplish his goal, Paperboy ran to the doors of PS 266. But before he entered the school, Billy grabbed his neck and started choking him again. Before he could stop Billy, he threw Paperboy to floor. Paperboy was getting tired of this. Plus, he was running out of time. Paperboy stood up and tried to kick Billy. Billy evaded the attack and tried to kick Paperboy. Paperboy dodged it and tried once again to kick Billy. Instead of evading the attack, Billy grabbed Paperboy's foot and said, "You should've been my friend, Paperboy."

With those words Billy swung Paperboy by his foot and let go. Paperboy flew in the air for seven seconds and crashed into the gate he chained the PaperMobile to with a big bang, and then crashed to the ground, right in front of the PaperMobile.

Billy stood there, and then started his strange hopping and smiling.

Paperboy lay there on the floor. With each second, his anger increased. Paperboy finally stood up. He ripped a paper airplane off his PaperMobile, put it between his fingers, and walked toward Billy. With each step Paperboy's anger grew.

Paperboy also could not see Billy clearly. He was dizzy; and every part of his body ached. But this could not stop him from walking toward Billy. Paperboy had also temporarily forgotten about Mr. Pride and Mr. Raptor. His only focus was Billy.

When Paperboy finally reached Billy, he channeled all the anger he had accumulated into his fist with the paper airplane and punched Billy on the right side of his face with all of his might. Billy flew to the gate and hit the same spot Paperboy did. Suddenly that piece of the gate broke and Billy fell through the gate and plunged to the ground. Paperboy waited to see if Billy would stand up. After two minutes, Billy got up. At that moment, Paperboy noticed a paper cut starting from Billy's right cheek and ending at his left nostril. Billy staggered toward Paperboy with a smile on his face.

When Billy was a few feet away from Paperboy, he said, "You went too far Paperboy. All I wanted was a friend. Just one friend! But nobody wants to be my friend. Nobody! But now, I know what I was meant for. I know what I have to do for all of you to appreciate me. From now on, I shall become a hunter. I shall be the Mad Hunter! And you Paperboy, have the honor of being my prey. Tomorrow at recess, I shall capture and slay the elusive Paperboy! And mark my words Paperboy, until I destroy you I will never give up the hunt! Never!"

With that Billy Howard ran away from PS 266.

Suddenly the school bell rang. Paperboy didn't make it in time. To make matters worse, Paperboy gave birth to a new enemy.

That punch must've destroyed whatever sense was left in Billy, Paperboy thought.

With fatigue and guilt weighing down his legs, Paperboy walked to the janitor's closet and changed. Michael then walked to class.

Mr. Raptor was extracting more information about Paperboy that day in class. Today Michael knew not to tell Mr. Raptor anything. He didn't want to make his situation worse than it already was. Michael also noticed Nina in back of him. They both said hello and went back to their boring day of class.

Then the bell rang for recess. Michael didn't even want to change into his Paperboy costume. He then remembered what happened two weeks ago. With those memories in mind, Michael went to the janitor's closet and changed. Paperboy only armed himself with two paper claws, one on each hand, and two paper airplanes, one on each hand between his pointer and middle finger.

Outside, Michael saw bullies everywhere. They were bullying the gossiping girls, game whiz boys, and the nerds. Paperboy didn't know where to start. He decided to stop the bullies from bullying the nerds. Paperboy ran over to the nerds and tapped a bully on the shoulder.

The bully turned around, looked at Paperboy, and shouted, "He's here!"

Suddenly all the bullies stopped. They turned and faced Paperboy. Then they turned toward the front of the playground. Paperboy turned towards them. He gasped. Walking toward Paperboy was Shorty Scarface. Paperboy didn't know what to do. He just stood there until Shorty reached him.

"I haven't seen you in a long time, Michael. We have a lot of catching up to do," he said in a low, controlled voice. Paperboy could tell Shorty was trying to contain his anger.

"You offended me beyond belief Michael," Shorty continued. "Now you're going to pay."

"You can't stop me, Shorty Scarface," Paperboy replied. "No matter what you do, I'm still going to destroy LOEP."

"LOEP will never die!" Shorty screamed.

"I'm glad you're here. Now I can finish what I started," Paperboy said. Shorty stared back angrily at Paperboy.

"Do you think you can get rid of LOEP so easily?" he said with a sneer. "Besides, ScizzorMan is not exactly gone. Michael, you seem to have a lot of trouble defeating ScizzorMan alone. Because of this, LOEP sent you a present. Prepare to meet your doom Michael. Meet the ScizzorMen!"

Suddenly three kids that looked exactly like ScizzorMan appeared. Each one had a scissor gun in his hand. Paperboy gasped.

"The ScizzorMan you fought was one of four identical quadruplets." Shorty explained. "These are the other three identical quadruplets. And all three of them are stronger than ScizzorMan. This is ScizzorMan A," Shorty said pointing to the kid with the letter "A" on his costume. "This is ScizzorMan B," Shorty said pointing to the kid with the letter "B" on his costume. "This is ScizzorMan C," Shorty said pointing to the kid with the letter "C" on his costume.

"You should never have offended me, Michael. ScizzorMen attack!"

With that, Shorty left Paperboy to face the ScizzorMen. Paperboy was not prepared for a fight like this. He was injured and had only his paper airplane and paper claw. The ScizzorMen charged at Paperboy. ScizzorMan A tackled Paperboy to the floor. The tackle was so powerful Paperboy dropped both paper airplanes.

Then that same boy picked Paperboy up and held him still, while the other two ScizzorMen aimed at Paperboy with their scissor guns.

Using his paper claw, Paperboy pierced the boy's wrist, setting himself free. He dropped to the ground as the other two ScizzorMen fired their scissor guns. Ploc! Ploc! Ploc! Ploc! The scissors rushed out of the scissor guns and hit ScizzorMan A.

"AHHHHHH!" He cried out in pain.

Paperboy stood up. ScizzorMan B punched Paperboy to the ground. He then aimed his scissor gun at Paperboy. Suddenly a protractor hit the scissor gun, knocking it out of ScizzorMan B's hand. Then a boy wearing a hockey mask and roller skates appeared.

The boy fired a protractor at each of the ScizzorMen's legs. Then ropes came out of the protractors and reached back to the boy in the hockey mask. The boy grabbed the three ropes and started skating, while the ScizzorMen dragged behind him. The boy set up three protractor traps while skating.

Paperboy recognized the boy in the hockey mask. It was James! After setting the protractor traps, James skated over to one of them. ScizzorMan A was caught in the trap, and he was still dragging behind James. James continued this until all the ScizzorMen were trapped.

James went over to where Paperboy kept the PaperMobile. A crowd followed him. Paperboy layed there, injured. James tied the three ropes he was holding in one strong knot. Then he climbed the gate and jumped to the other side, the ScizzorMen still hanging on the opposite side.

James tied the rope to the gate in a strong knot. He then climbed to the other side and set up three protractor traps right under the ScizzorMen who were hanging from the gate upside down. The crowd cheered, as James went back and helped Paperboy up and to his PaperMobile.

While the ScizzorMen struggled to release themselves, Paperboy rode home to safety, with the help of his friend. Shorty Scarface was furious. He told all the bullies to go back to LOEP's base. Then he stood before the ScizzorMen and said, "Get back to base now."

When Michael got home, he changed out of his costume and started tending to his injuries. Paperboy failed. If James didn't save him, Michael would've been dead. Unfortunately for Michael, this was just the beginning. Mr. Raptor was after him, Shorty Scarface was after him, and tomorrow he would become prey to his own creation. It was more than Michael could bear. Michael sighed. There was little left he could do. He just had to heal fast. Michael sighed again. No matter how he looked at it, he knew it, Billy knew it, Max knew it, and Mr. Raptor knew it: The destruction of Paperboy was near.

Chapter 6
The Mad Hunter

AGENDA FOR TODAY

READING LIST

HOMEWORK

REPORTS DUE

SIX

Michael got up the next morning with a tormenting headache. He had not made a complete recovery from yesterday, but he was well enough to face the Mad Hunter today. After his morning routine he changed into his Paperboy costume. He also put an excessive amount of paper lasers, PBB's, paper airplanes, and paper claws in his knapsack. Paperboy then took out the PaperMobile from the garage and rode to PS 266.

He entered PS 266 and hastily ran to the janitor's closet and changed back to Michael.

When he walked into class, Miss Rex was there, and the chalkboard was full of work. Michael finished his work swiftly. Soon the bell rang for recess. Michael quickly changed in the janitor's closet. Paperboy walked out, ready to face his new enemy.

This time he was armed with everything. He had two paper airplanes, (one on each hand between his pointer and middle finger); four paper lasers, (two in his front pockets and two in his back pockets); four PBB's, (two on each hand between his middle finger, pointer finger, and pinky); and two paper claws, (one on each hand). Paperboy walked out to the school playground.

Outside, Paperboy didn't see Billy or bullies. Then a game whiz boy ran to him.

"I heard you were hurt yesterday. Are you okay?" the game whiz boy asked.

"Yes, I'm fine," Paperboy replied.

Paperboy was surprised. Every group except the bullies seemed to really care about him. Suddenly a pencil struck the boy's body.

"OHHHHHH!" He cried out in pain.

Paperboy was alarmed. *Where did that pencil come from?* Suddenly Paperboy was kicked to the ground, and the game whiz boy was snatched from the ground by a mysterious figure. Paperboy chased the figure to the back of the playground. The figure dropped the boy and turned around. It was Billy!

Billy smiled and said, "If you want to save your friend, you face me, the Mad Hunter, in a fight to the death."

The terms were insane, but Paperboy had no choice.

"I accept," he replied.

"Then let the slaying of my prey begin!" The Mad Hunter announced.

Suddenly James appeared in his hockey mask and roller skates. He fired a protractor at the Mad Hunter. The Mad Hunter dodged it, and took out a ruler with a rope tied onto it. He put a pencil on the rope, aimed for James' leg, pulled back the rope, and fired. The Mad Hunter was using the ruler like a bow and the pencil like an arrow! The pencil penetrated James' leg.

"OWWW!" James cried out in pain.

Before James could do anything else, the Mad Hunter picked him up and threw him seven feet in the air. He fired pencils at James until he hit the ground. The Mad Hunter then pulled out a scissor and said,

"Never disturb me from my hunt."

James, wounded and injured from his attacker, could not fight back. Just before the Mad Hunter was going to attack James, a PBB hit his hand, forcing him to drop his scissor. Paperboy then turned the Mad Hunter around to face him and attacked the Mad Hunter with a paper airplane. Before the mad Hunter could react, Paperboy grabbed him with his paper claw (which pierced the Mad Hunter) and threw him in the opposite direction of James.

The Mad Hunter landed on the ground with a thud. He then got up and charged toward Paperboy. Before he reached him, Paperboy threw another PBB at the Mad Hunter. While the Mad Hunter reacted to this attack, Paperboy took out and fired his paper laser.

"AHHHHHH!" The Mad Hunter cried out in pain.

Paperboy ran over to the Mad Hunter and attacked him with his paper airplane. Then he pushed the Mad Hunter to the floor with his paper claw (which pierced the Mad Hunter). He picked up a wounded Mad Hunter with his paper claw and threw him to a nearby wall, close to where the game whiz boy was. The Mad Hunter hit the wall hard and bounced off the wall, landing on the ground. The Mad Hunter could barely lift a finger. Paperboy picked up the Mad Hunter's scissor and went over to the Mad Hunter.

"A fight to the death was a crazy idea," Paperboy said triumphantly. "Lucky for you I'm not the kind of person to kill anyone or anything. I'm confiscating this scissor and I'm leaving you here to think about what you did. You lost, so I'm also taking the game whiz boy with me. I hope you never try anything like this again, Mad Hunter."

With that, Paperboy led the game whiz boy to the front of the playground. Paperboy had won today; and he had regained something important. He had regained his faith in himself. It was the only thing that kept him alive with a purpose, and Paperboy vowed to himself never to lose his faith again.

Unfortunately for Paperboy, Mr. Raptor had seen his fight with the Mad Hunter. Mr. Raptor ignored what the Mad Hunter had done and looked at what Paperboy had done to the Mad Hunter. The Mad Hunter had paper cuts on almost every part of his body. This was just further proof to Mr. Raptor that Paperboy had to be captured.

Later that day Mr. Raptor called an old friend of his. He told his friend about Paperboy and his friend promised to be there tomorrow to " exterminate Paperboy." Mr. Raptor smiled. He was going to get rid of Paperboy, and he was going to do it with or without the principal's permission.

Chapter 7
The Merciless School Guard

SEVEN

The next day Michael got up with a lot of energy. He immediately started getting ready for school. When he arrived at school, Miss Rex was there again that day, and the chalkboard was yet again filled with work. Michael started his work. Before he finished, Nina tapped him on the shoulder. Michael turned around.

"What is it?" Michael whispered.

"Don't change into Paperboy today," Nina warned. "Mr. Raptor..."

"Nina!" Miss Rex interrupted. "Finish your work in the back of the classroom. Michael, turn around and finish your work."

Nina moved to the back of the classroom and Michael turned around and thought about what Nina said.

There's no reason not to turn into Paperboy. I made a promise to every group except the bullies and I have to keep it.

Michael finished his work. The bell rang. It was time for recess. Michael changed into Paperboy and then went outside to recess. Paperboy had his normal amount of weapons. He had two paper airplanes (in their normal positions); two Paper claws, (one on each hand); two PBB's, (one on each hand between his middle and pointer finger); and two paper lasers, (one in each of his two front pockets).

Once Paperboy was outside, he saw no bullies, no Mad Hunter, and no Shorty Scarface. However, he did see Mr. Raptor. This was his chance to lose an enemy. Paperboy walked over to Mr. Raptor. Once Mr. Raptor saw him, he shouted, " Paperboy's here!"

Paperboy ignored this and said, "Mr. Raptor, I have to talk to you."

Mr. Raptor ignored his plea. "I didn't get you the first time, but my plan won't fail this time. There he is. Paperboy I'd like you to meet a friend of mine. He was fired from his job as a school guard because he attacked a student. And now I hired him to get you. Turn around and say goodbye to your career of evil."

Paperboy couldn't believe it. This man was crazier than the Mad Hunter. Paperboy turned around and gasped. He couldn't believe his eyes. Walking toward Paperboy was a 7 ft. tall man with muscles bulging out of almost every part of his body. He had big, calloused hands and a frown on his face.

This is what Nina had warned him about. Once Paperboy saw this man, he knew what he had to do: run. Paperboy ran away from Mr. Raptor and ran toward the PaperMobile. The ground started rumbling, and Paperboy knew that man was chasing after him.

Paperboy ran to the PaperMobile and struggled to unlock it. Once Paperboy had unlocked it, a cold, hard hand grabbed his neck. The hand tightened around Paperboy's neck, choking him. Paperboy was picked up off the ground and was turned to face the terrible man behind him.

"You must be Paperboy." the man said. "I've heard a lot about you."

The man threw Paperboy to the floor. Paperboy landed hard on the cold ground. Before Paperboy could get up, the man picked him up and threw him into the air. In midair, Paperboy balanced himself upright and threw a PBB at the man.

The man cried out in pain. Once Paperboy was on the same level as the man's face, he grabbed the man's face with his Paper claw. The man tried to shake Paperboy off his face, but Paperboy hung on. It was a long way down. The man backed up, and a second later he was wrapped up in ropes. The man fell.

James is here. Paperboy thought.

Paperboy jumped off the man and ran toward the PaperMobile. Suddenly the man broke the ropes he was bound by, and took out the two small protractors that were in his foot. Paperboy pedaled to Mr.

Raptor as the man stood up.

As Paperboy pedaled, the ground started to shake. All at once the PaperMobile was lifted off the ground. Paperboy turned and fired his last PBB. The man lifted the PaperMobile, and caught the PBB with his other hand before it hit his face. He then extended the arm that was holding the PaperMobile and threw the PaperMobile, with Paperboy on it, as far as he could.

Paperboy was traveling at a very high speed covering many feet. He could see every group except the bullies below him for a second as he zoomed past them. Paperboy didn't dare to jump. He was too high. He just had to wait until he hit the ground. Paperboy crashed in front of the playground. Even as Paperboy lay injured on the ground, he could feel the ground shaking. That man was coming to finish him off. Paperboy didn't want to get up. Even lifting a finger hurt him. His whole body ached. But Paperboy could not give up. He would never give up.

Paperboy stood up, trying to ignore the pain. Suddenly the ground stopped shaking. A huge shadow loomed over Paperboy. The man was here. He picked up Paperboy and said, "This is the end, Paperboy."

Out of the corner of his eye, Paperboy spotted James on the roof. James jumped off, feet extended at the man's face. James hit the man and the man lost his balance, dropping Paperboy. Paperboy landed on the ground. Despite his pain, he continued to fight, as the determined man still tried to grab him.

The man managed to wrap a heavy hand around him, but Paperboy was determined not to let this man overpower him. Paperboy pierced the man's wrist with his paper claw. The man cried out in pain and loosened his grip on him. As the man stood up, several protractors pierced his foot and ropes bound his body. The man fell again.

By this time, James had set up protractor traps all around the man. Paperboy grabbed his PaperMobile and pedaled away from the playground before the man broke out of his second protractor trap. Paperboy pedaled home, weakened and bruised, but his will strong and unharmed.

Mr. Raptor had watch the entire fight and was furious at the outcome. He turned around to go inside. Instead, he found an angry Mr. Pride behind him. Mr. Raptor was in deep trouble.

At home Paperboy thought about what he had done. He then thought about all of his enemies. He had to do something to persuade his enemies to see his point of view. He could persuade Mr. Raptor, find someone to help Billy, and destroy LOEP (The League of Evil People). There was no remedy for LOEP; Paperboy had to destroy it. He had to do this before the organization got any stronger.

Tomorrow I'm going to eliminate one of my enemies, Paperboy thought as he began to plan for the destruction of LOEP.

Chapter 8
The Scizzormen Return

EIGHT

The next day Michael figured out how he was going to destroy LOEP. First, Michael would go to school. He should have no enemies during recess. Paperboy had defeated Shorty Scarface, the Mad Hunter, and Mr. Raptor. After school, Michael would change into Paperboy again and go downtown. Michael remembered where LOEP's original base was; he just hoped they had not changed their location. Paperboy would then infiltrate the base, and destroy LOEP inside out. His plan could not fail.

With these thoughts in mind, Michael started getting ready for school.

In his classroom, Miss Rex was there, but there was no work on the chalk board. As soon as Michael took his seat, Miss Rex shouted, "Pop quiz!"

The class groaned as Miss Rex passed out the quiz to her students. Michael finished his quiz accurately and swiftly. Once the class was dismissed, Michael changed into his Paperboy costume. He armed himself with two paper airplanes, two paper claws, two PBB's, and two paper lasers. The paper airplanes and paper claws were in their normal positions, and there was one PBB in each of Paperboy's hands. The paper lasers were in each of Paperboy's front pockets. Paperboy walked out to recess.

Outside, Paperboy saw bullies holding back school guards, and the other three groups were in one corner of the playground.

"*What's going on?*" Paperboy wondered.

Paperboy ran to the corner of the playground where the other three groups were. Once he was there, Paperboy was pushed to the ground. When Paperboy looked up to see who pushed him, he saw ScizzorMan C. Paperboy was shocked. LOEP was trying to destroy him again? Then he saw his old enemy Shorty Scarface.

"Pull him up," Shorty commanded.

ScizzorMan C pulled Paperboy up, and held his arms tightly.

"You can't pull any tricks on us this time Paperboy," Shorty said firmly. "Just when we were about to destroy you, your friend appeared and ruined my plan. But that won't happen this time. We captured your friend, and while we were at it, we decided to take off his mask too. James Pace made a big mistake. But he will pay for his mistake."

"Where is he?" Paperboy demanded.

"He's busy right now," Shortly replied. "Over there."

Shorty pointed to the gate Paperboy had chained his PaperMobile to. James was hanging upside down from a rope with his mask off. James looked like he had taken a stroll through a meadow of pain. There was a bully under James, watching him very carefully.

"James!" Paperboy cried out.

Paperboy tried to run to James, but he forgot that one of the ScizzorMen was holding him.

"Now Paperboy," Shorty said happily. "You have nobody to save you. You'll face and perish from the wrath of the mighty ScizzorMen!"

With that Shorty left Paperboy alone to face his fate. Suddenly the other two ScizzorMen appeared with two scissor guns in their hands. Once they were in firing range, they aimed at Paperboy. Paperboy pierced ScizzorMan C and dropped to the ground. As the two ScizzorMen fired, Paperboy jumped out of the way of the scissors. Paperboy ran over to the other two ScizzorMen and attacked them using his paper airplane.

The two ScizzorMen cried out in pain.

Paperboy tried to run and save James. But before he could make it to the gate, ScizzorMan B grabbed his arm and swung Paperboy away from the gate. Paperboy landed hard on the ground. As Paperboy tried to stand up, ScizzorMan A tackled him from behind, knocking him back to the ground. Paperboy was getting frustrated. He needed to save James.

ScizzorMan A pulled out two scissor guns and aimed at Paperboy. Suddenly, Paperboy extended his left leg and turned to the right quickly. ScizzorMan A was in the way of Paperboy's leg and he was hit before he fired the two scissor guns.

Paperboy stood up quickly and pierced ScizzorMan A's wrist with his paper claw, forcing the ScizzorMan to drop his two scissor guns. Paperboy quickly picked them up and ran to help James. The three ScizzorMen followed him. Paperboy threw two PBB's at two of the ScizzorMen. The two ScizzorMen stopped and cried out in pain. While running, Paperboy looked back, aimed and fired a scissor from one of the scissor guns. The scissor hit the last ScizzorMan, and the ScizzorMan cried out in pain.

Paperboy finally reached James. Before the bully guarding James could react, Paperboy attacked him with his paper airplane. He grabbed the startled boy with his paper claw and threw him out of his way. Paperboy quickly climbed to James.

"Are you okay?" Paperboy asked.

"I could be better," James replied painfully.

"I'm going to get you out of here James. When I free you, cling to the gate and climb down. I'm going to unlock my bike and I want you to pedal out of here."

Paperboy freed James and unlocked the PaperMobile. James quickly rode away to safety. But Paperboy had little time to enjoy his success because the ScizzorMen suddenly reappeared. Paperboy had little left to fight with. He only had two scissors left. How could he evade all of the ScizzorMen this time? But Paperboy had no choice but to face the three mighty ScizzorMen. Paperboy ran to the ScizzorMen.

Just as Paperboy was about to attack, someone grabbed him from behind. Instinctively, Paperboy used his paper claw. However, the person had already raised his fist. As Paperboy turned to face his attacker, his attacker struck. Then everything in Paperboy's world went black.

Chapter 9
The House Of Horror

NINE

When Paperboy woke up, he found himself in a long hallway. Rays of light shined through the long windows on the walls.

Where am I? Paperboy wondered.

Paperboy walked around the hallway. He noticed two paper airplanes on the floor. He also noticed he did not have his. Were these his? Paperboy looked at the paper airplane. It was as sharp as one he would have constructed. This must have been his. Paperboy checked to see what weapons he did have. He had both his paper lasers and both his paper claws. However, he had no scissor guns.

As Paperboy checked for PBB's, he remembered he used them against the ScizzorMen. A question popped into his head: *Where are the ScizzorMen?* Paperboy noticed a clock on the wall. The time was 7:30. He was confused. Wasn't that the time he got ready to go to school? Paperboy needed to get out of this house and go home. He still had a headache from whoever had hit him. He saw a door at the end of the hallway.

Maybe that's the way out of here, Paperboy hoped.

Paperboy put each paper airplane on his hand (between his pointer and middle finger) and walked to the door. Paperboy opened the door. Inside was a wide hallway with a door at the end.

"This might take awhile," Paperboy said sadly.

Meanwhile, James got up and started preparing to go to school. He had not made a complete recovery from yesterday, but he was well enough to go to school. Like his friend Michael, he had received a real, painful dose of what it really means to be a hero.

At school, he would give Michael back his bike and thank him for saving him. He wondered if Michael was okay. He hoped he was alive and had defeated the ScizzorMen.

With these thoughts in mind, James started getting ready for school. James took a shower, got dressed, went downstairs and said good morning to his mother and father, and then ate the breakfast his mother had made for him. James took out Michael's bike from his garage and rode to PS 266. He chained Michael's bike to the gate, then walked to class.

Meanwhile, Paperboy was having no luck leaving the strange house he was in. He had been through ten rooms already. Paperboy walked down another hallway and reached the door at the end. He opened the door. Suddenly, a pencil fell from the ceiling. Paperboy moved forward to evade the pencil. Suddenly another pencil came down from the ceiling above Paperboy.

Paperboy decided to run to the next door. As Paperboy ran, pencils came crashing down behind him. When he finally reached the door, he opened it quickly before the pencils hit him. Paperboy entered the next room as he heard the pencils hit the ground.

What was that all about? Paperboy wondered as he walked to the next door. As Paperboy neared the next door, the walls and ceilings opened up and fired sharp scissors all around the room. Paperboy tried to run to the door, but was hit three times before he reached the door.

Paperboy opened the door and ran in. This was getting serious. He had to get out of here before he was killed. Paperboy walked to the next door. He heard a hissing sound close to the door. As Paperboy neared the door, the floor he was standing on collapsed and he fell into a small hole. In the hole was a 5 ft. long poisonous snake!

Paperboy tried to stay calm as the snake slithered toward him. He tried to climb out of the hole, but he was unsuccessful. Paperboy took out a paper laser. The snake stood back, appearing ready to strike. Paperboy fired the paper laser again and again, which stopped the snake in its tracks. Paperboy kept firing the paper laser. It was the only thing keeping him alive.

Meanwhile, James did his work in class until the bell rang for recess. James then grabbed his hockey mask and roller skates from his knapsack and put them on in the boys' bathroom. He then skated out of the bathroom and to recess. Outside, there seemed to be no bullies, Mad Hunter, or Mr. Raptor. James did see Nina, and he skated toward her.

"Hi Nina," James called. "Have you seen Michael?"

"He wasn't here today," Nina replied.

James was worried now. Did the ScizzorMen capture Michael? Michael would come today for his bike. *Why wasn't he here?* James had to find him.

"I think something happened to Michael," James said worriedly. "I have to find him. And I don't think I can do it alone. Could you please help me Nina? Just this once?"

"I'll see what I can do," Nina answered.

"That's what you always say!" James said angrily. "Then you go talk to your friends. I've asked you to help me help Paperboy since we got to this school. You never came once! This time, Michael might be in trouble. He probably needs our help. So for one day, could you forget your friends and help save Michael?"

"Only if you have proof he's in trouble," Nina answered calmly.

"Forget it!" James roared. "You only care about talking while Michael and I are trying to save the school from being taken over by the wrong people. I don't need your..."

"Fine!" Nina interrupted. "I'll help you. What do we have to do?"

"We'll start at Michael's house," James replied. "Let's go."

James and Nina departed from PS 266 and went to Michael's house.

Meanwhile, Paperboy was still distracting the snake with his paper laser. He needed to get out of this hole and out of this house. Paperboy had an idea. He stopped firing his paper laser. As the snake came toward him, Paperboy grabbed the snake below his head. He opened the snake's mouth, exposing its fangs.

He threw the snake, with its fangs exposed, to the part of the hole he could not reach. The snake's fangs hooked to the hole in the wall. Paperboy then grabbed the snake's tail and started climbing out of the hole.

When Paperboy was out of the hole, he sighed in relief.

Meanwhile, James and Nina climbed into one of Michael's open windows and looked around his room for clues. They found nothing.

"He must be with the ScizzorMen," James said. "We have to go to their base. But I don't know where it is."

James looked out the window in defeat. Then he saw a boy who looked like a bully walking away from Michael's house. James had to follow him.

"Follow me Nina," James instructed.

James climbed out of Michael's window and followed the bully. Nina followed James.

Meanwhile, Paperboy walked to the door and opened it. What Paperboy saw made him sigh in disbelief. Standing in the middle of a big room with ropes hanging from the ceiling was the Mad Hunter; and he looked ready for battle.

Chapter 10
The Hunter vs. The Hunter

TEN

Paperboy could not believe this. He spared the Mad Hunter's life and now the Mad Hunter was trying to destroy him again.

"You look a little confused," the Mad Hunter said happily. "Allow me to make things clear to you before I destroy you. Ever since you had beaten me in our fight, I knew I was underestimating you. But I would not do that anymore. After awhile I was able to walk. Once I was able to walk, I thought of a way to destroy you.

"I walked to the train station and took a train downtown. When I got off the train, I walked downtown, still trying to figure out a way to finally capture and slay my prey. I then happened to walk by an abandoned factory. Then an idea finally came to me. I went in the factory and started redesigning it. This took a few days. But after I was done, I had turned the factory into a house of traps.

"Yes, I caused those pencils to fall. I caused the scissors to come out of the ceiling and walls. And I put a poisonous snake under the floor. All of the traps were set. All I needed was my prey. The next day I went to PS 266 to find you fighting boys with scissors.

"I grabbed you from behind and knocked you out before you had a chance to fight back. I carried you away from the boys with scissors and put you at the beginning of my house of traps."

The Mad Hunter paused for a moment to let Paperboy soak it all in.

"*Wow*," Paperboy thought, "*This guy really is a genius!*"

Almost as if he was reading Paperboy's mind, the Mad Hunter continued, "I carried you away from those boys with the scissors before they could do anything to stop me."

"It took you a day to wake up. I had also taken some weapons you had dropped and placed them in the house. A hunter only feels proud when he knows that he has defeated his prey at its strongest. You then managed to make it here; to the room of your demise. I must congratulate you. I didn't think you'd make it. But this is the end.

"Oh yes, I have one more surprise for you. I have a match and a matchbox in my pocket."

The Mad Hunter took out the match and the matchbox. He lit a match and threw it at the back of the room.

"We will now fight until the last one is standing. And if we don't finish the fight fast enough, we will both be burned to ashes. If a hunter cannot slay his prey, then he shall die with his prey."

Paperboy was speechless. He didn't know what to do. He could not believe the Mad Hunter would do this. Paperboy had to act fast. He had to put the match out. Paperboy tried to run past the Mad Hunter to the match, but once he was in the Mad Hunter's reach, the Mad Hunter grabbed him and threw him back to the wall.

Paperboy hit the wall, bounced off, and landed on the floor. The Mad Hunter then came charging at Paperboy. Paperboy then charged at the Mad Hunter, not sure if he could defeat the Mad Hunter and stop the fire.

Meanwhile, James and Nina followed the bully downtown. The bully turned into an alley. James and Nina turned into the same alley just in time to see the bully go into a nearby building's window. He then saw a rope come up and go into the building. James sighed. How was he going to get into the building to save Paperboy?

"Any ideas?" James asked.

"None," Nina replied.

Meanwhile, the fight with Paperboy and the Mad Hunter raged on. The fire was quickly spreading, almost covering the whole back of the room and ready to charge forward. Paperboy attacked the Mad Hunter with his paper airplane. The Mad Hunter retaliated with a tackle to the floor.

The Mad Hunter got up, went back a few steps, and took a pencil and his ruler with a rope on it. He aimed at Paperboy and fired. Paperboy barely evaded the pencil. He stood up and ran to the Mad Hunter. Before he reached the Mad Hunter, the Mad Hunter took out another pencil, pulled the rope back, and fired. Paperboy was unable to dodge this pencil, and the pencil hit him.

Paperboy cried out in pain just before another pencil hit him. After that, another pencil hit Paperboy. The Mad Hunter fired pencils mercilessly until Paperboy fell to the ground. The Mad Hunter picked up Paperboy and threw him in the direction of the flames. Paperboy fell inches from the hot flames. Paperboy tried to get up, but the Mad Hunter forced him back down with his lethal pencils.

After being hit with pencils ten times, Paperboy stayed down. Paperboy knew flames were coming towards him, but he didn't know what to do. The Mad Hunter ran over to a wall and pulled a hidden lever. Suddenly the middle of the room opened up, revealing a deep hole with sharpened pencils at the bottom. A nearby rope that was hanging from the ceiling descended to the ground.

The Mad Hunter grabbed a groggy Paperboy and dragged him to the rope. He tied Paperboy's hands to the rope, went over to the wall, and pulled the lever again. The rope rose to the ceiling, with Paperboy tied to it. The rope moved over to the hole and stopped. The Mad Hunter smiled. The flames had covered half the room by now, and had weakened the ceiling. Some parts of the ceiling at the back of the room had fallen.

The Mad Hunter shouted at the top of his lungs, "Now for the destruction of my formidable and elusive prey, Paperboy!"

Meanwhile, while trying to figure out how to get into the building, James heard the Mad Hunter's shout. He was immediately alarmed.

"We are at the wrong place, Nina," James said quickly. "Paperboy is at the source of that shout. We have to follow where the voice came from immediately!"

James skated to the voice's source. Nina followed him. James and Nina had finally made it to the abandoned factory.

"He's in here," James said quickly.

He opened the door and skated inside. Nina followed him. James skated at full speed through ten rooms, and as hard as it was, Nina followed him. James then skated through the room filled with pencils, through the room filled with scissors, and stopped at the door in the room with the snake. Nina ran in the room and to James, completely out of breath. James could make out a cackling sound coming from the next room.

"He's in there," James said quietly. "Okay Nina. We are going to go inside quietly and try to save Paperboy and judging by the words, stop the Mad Hunter."

"No," Nina said at her normal voice. "I helped you make it here and that's all I'm going to do. You're on your own from here. Downtown is too dangerous. I'm going back to PS 266."

"What!" James whispered. "Fine. I don't need you. Go. I can handle this by myself."

James opened the door and skated inside, leaving the door open. He saw Paperboy's hands tied to a rope above a hole of sharpened pencils. The Mad Hunter was firing pencils at Paperboy. In spite of the pain it caused him, Paperboy swung on the rope to dodge the pencils. There was also a fire behind Paperboy that was slowly devouring the room.

James skated to the Mad Hunter and tackled him to the ground. Before the Mad Hunter could react to this attack, James picked him up and threw him against a nearby wall. The Mad Hunter hit the wall, bounced off, and landed on the floor. He got up.

James rushed the Mad Hunter for another attack, but the Mad Hunter hit James with a pencil before he reached him. James cried out in pain. The Mad Hunter then tackled him to the floor. He picked James up and threw him into the hole. James reacted quickly, clinging to the edge. The Mad Hunter took a pencil, put it on the ruler, pulled the rope back, aimed, and said, "I warned you once, but now you'll never forget. Never interrupt me from my hunt!"

It looked hopeless. Paperboy's hands were tied to a rope on the ceiling. Eventually, the fire would weaken the ceiling and Paperboy would fall into the hole. James was hanging on by the edge of the hole, and the Mad Hunter was about to make him lose his grip and fall in the hole. The Mad Hunter then fired his pencil.

Suddenly a voice behind the Mad Hunter shouted, "NOOOOOOOO!"

A large blast of water hit the pencil before it hit James. The person who had saved James came into clearer view. It was Nina! Nina kicked the Mad Hunter to the ground.

She raised her hand out to James and said, "I changed my mind."

James grabbed her hand and Nina pulled him out of danger. The Mad Hunter struggled to stand up. Nina kicked him back down and stood before Paperboy.

"How can I get you down?" she asked Paperboy.

"The wall to your right," Paperboy replied.

Nina looked at the wall and found the secret lever. She pulled it and the rope holding Paperboy moved out from above the hole and above Nina. Nina stood back as the rope descended to the floor. Nina then untied Paperboy.

Paperboy was in tears. His friends had come to his rescue. They had saved him because they were true friends and they would not let him die if it could be prevented.

The Mad Hunter finally was able to get back on his feet. Paperboy couldn't believe it. But this time he wasn't the one outnumbered. Paperboy, James, and Nina charged at the Mad Hunter to overpower him. James then attacked the Mad Hunter with a protractor and threw him away from Nina to Paperboy's feet. The Mad Hunter managed to fire two pencils stopping James and Nina, but did not have enough time to fire another pencil before Paperboy reached him. Paperboy attacked the Mad Hunter fiercely with his paper air planes. He then grabbed the Mad Hunter with his paper claws and swung him to the other side of the room. There was not much of the room that had not been conquered by the flames. James and Nina then ran to the Man Hunter. The Mad Hunter tripped Nina and said, "Now you're going to pay. You're my prey from now on."

"Do you give up?" Paperboy asked.

"Yes," the Mad Hunter replied.

"Then let's get out of here."

"Aren't you angry at me?" The Mad Hunter asked.

"The last time I got angry at someone, I created a monster. I'm not doing that again," Paperboy replied.

The Mad Hunter reached out and grabbed Paperboy's legs.

"You're too generous," he said.

The Mad Hunter tried to trip Paperboy, But he was not quick enough. Paperboy easily evaded his effort. The Mad Hunter then prepared to swing at Paperboy but Paperboy pierced his hand with a paper claw.

"You haven't changed at all," Paperboy said as he picked the Mad Hunter up and threw him to James. However, Nina intercepted the throw and threw the Mad Hunter into the hole. The Mad Hunter reacted quickly and hung on to the edge of the hole. But the fire had weakened the ceiling and a piece of the ceiling fell onto the Mad Hunter's hand. The Mad Hunter let go of the edge unwillingly and fell into the hole.

"NOOOOOO!" The Mad Hunter cried as he fell into his own trap. Paperboy didn't even want to look at what happened to the Mad Hunter.

"Let's get out of here!" Nina screamed. "The whole room is almost up in flames!"

Nina and James ran out of the room. Reluctantly, Paperboy ran out too. Nina, James, and Paperboy ran out of the room with the snake, out of the room that was filled with scissors, out of the room that was filled with pencils, out of the ten rooms, and finally out of the hallway and out of the house.

Once they were out of the house, the three friends sighed in relief. After Paperboy and Nina caught their breath, they went to the train station and caught a train going uptown. On the train, the three friends talked. Then Paperboy asked Nina the question that was really bothering him.

"Why did you throw the Mad Hunter into the hole, Nina?" Paperboy asked.

"Because he wasn't going to change," Nina answered. "He was taking advantage of you. Plus the room was up in flames!"

"Okay," Paperboy answered. "I guess you're right."

When the train finally arrived at their stop, Paperboy, James, and Nina got off the train and out of the train station.

"I'm going home," Paperboy said. "I have a lot of sleep to catch up on."

"Recess is over," Nina said. "We might as well all go home."

"Okay," James replied. "I'll ride your bike back to your house, Michael."

"Thanks," Paperboy answered. "And thank you for all the times you helped me."

"No problem," James and Nina said in unison.

With that, Paperboy, James, and Nina went their separate ways. As much as Paperboy was hurt, he felt great. He had overcome the odds more than once, and the best thing was: he had friends to help him! Paperboy felt like he could take on anything, as long as he had James and Nina. Nothing could stop him. Unfortunately, somebody yards behind him didn't think this way.

Omari Jeremiah:
Omari Jeremiah is a 14-year old African-American teenager from the Bronx, New York. He attended elementary school at CES 109 in the Bronx. It was there that his tremendous writing ability began to surface. He received many awards for Creative Writing from CES 109. He then attended Arturo Toscanni Community Junior High School 145 in the Bronx and graduated with honors in 2004. Omari also attended the Fieldson Enrichment Program (FEP) which is a special program for academically gifted students. Omari, a 9th grade student, presently attends the Hackley School in Tarrytown, New York.

From a very early age, Omari has shown a keen interest in writing. He has written many short stories and poems. He wrote his first published book, "Paperboy" when he was only 12 years old. This book has received many accolades and has propelled Omari into the spotlight. He has been in numerous newspapers across the country, and abroad, as well as interviewed on many radio and television stations.

He wrote Paperboy 2 when he was 13 years old. In the summer of 2004, at the age of 14, he completed the other four books in the Paperboy series. Omari believes that writing is a way to express your feelings, your internal emotions and your creativity in a way nobody can question.

He is also an avid reader and his other interest and hobbies include fencing, playing the alto saxophone and table tennis. Omari hopes to grow up to be a professional author, fencer and saxophonist.

He currently resides in the Bronx with his parents, an older sister and an older brother.

Bernie Rollins:
Bernard (Bernie)Rollins, a California-based artist, designer and art director, created the illustrations for Paperboy II. A New Yorker by birth, from age 5, Bernie drew comic books. When approached by Morton Books with the concept of Paperboy, he remembered his own childhood drawing comic books at the kitchen table. He felt that helping the author make his story visual was just the way things were supposed to happen.

"It felt right and I had fun doing it," he admits.

Rollins currently works for a Los Angeles newspaper chain.